3 PLUSFURY OUR STORY

By Pamela Baker

Illustrated by Book writer corner

DEDICATION

This book is dedicated to my beautiful children and grandchildren, With a special shout out to all the people that work with dogs and train dogs, as well as rescue dogs, each and every one of you has a part in saving these beautiful creatures. Opening your heart to a dog makes a huge difference. I've learned so much from adopting these beautiful dogs. I have been shown bravery love and compassion and mostly patience. Dogs dedicate their lives to us with unconditional love and loyalty. When we give them the right tools to learn and be a part of our family they give us everything in return. I hope by sharing this you will consider giving a dog a home.

Thank you all for your love.

Pamela – Mama Lita

Tony

Kody

Roxy

fury

3 PLUS FURY

ESTABLISHED 2023

It had rained all morning. It was very cold. Tony, a beautiful tricolor German Shepherd, was running towards the concrete pad that was located in front of the farmhouse. Farmer Kurt split open the bag of dog food and poured it on the concrete pad. Kody and Tony were racing to get to the food before their sister Lucy. Kody was the taller of the two brothers. They were running neck and neck. Lucy was never nice to them and liked to eat all the food and drink all the water. She sprinted and ran past them laughing. She got to the concrete pad first. She ate every last drop of food. leaving nothing for Kody and Tony. Tony said to Kody, "Lucy did it again; another night of hunger". Tony put his paw on Kody and said to his brother. It's ok we will find something to nibble on. As he said it his stomach groweled loudly. He tried to smile through the pangs of hunger.

They both knew there would be nothing until tomorrow. They pretended it would be ok. It was the second night of no food. It would be a long night.

There is mom and dad, Kody, Tony, and Lucy. We lived on the farm with Farmer Kurt. Farmer Kurt was a tall man who always ran around and murmured under his breath. He never really talked to us, He mostly yelled at us and everyone else. Our days, were spent running around, playing in the mud, and or eating anything we could find in the yard. We liked to chase the goats even though we weren't allowed. When we chased the goats, he would yell at us. One day when we were chasing the goats , we got a little too close and farmer Kurt yelled , "that's it, you have to go." Go where Tony thought. He was scared and confused.

The next day we met farmer Yarth, He always drove a big red truck, sometimes with a trailer. He was a very tall man with a very loud scary voice. Who always wore work clothes or coveralls, a hat, and sunglasses. His clothes were always bright colors. He walked with a limp. He hardly ever smiled. Kody would sometimes hide when he heardhis truck.

Today, he said, "You're coming with me Tony. Then he put me in his truck." I looked at Kody and Lucy and wondered why he only took me. Kody ran behind the truck, I could see him running and getting smaller and smaller as we were leaving the yard. I wondered when I would see my brother Kody and sister Lucy again. I would miss Kody. He and I were together all the time. When it was cold we huddled together. We'd sit in the field and talk for hours. At night we slept side-by-side in the tall grass to keep warm. Lucy got to sleep inside. Kody and I knew it was because Lucy has perfect ears. Her ears stood straight up. Farmer Kurt always made fun of our ears. You see German shepherds ears should stand up. Ours were floppy and would not stand. We never wondered why Farmer Kurt didn't like us. Farmer Kurt would tell us that we were ugly. We never felt like we belonged at Farmer Kurt's. It had always been Kody and I protecting each other. Tony was so worried. He wondered where his brother was? He thought, is he still at the farm? Where was I going, Tony thought.

Farmer Yarth said we're here. You're going to live with Mama Lita. I was so confused I didn't know what was happening or why I wasn't going back to the farm? Where was my brother Kody? What was happening? I looked out the window to see a cute little gray house. It had lots of plants everywhere. I saw rows of beautiful almond trees. Tony closed his eyes and just kept repeating , please let them love me, please let them want me, please let them be nice. Please let them not care that my ears don't stand up.

Mama Lita gave Yarth a great big hug and called him boo bear. Tony laughed silently. He thought it was funny. Mama Lita was a tall lady with dark curly hair, big brown eyes and long eyelashes. She wore bright red lipstick, and a red bandanna in her hair. Red high-top shoes with white laces. She had a great big beautiful smile. She looked at me and said, well "Hello handsome, welcome home." I was so confused. Was this my new home? where was Kody? Mama Lita looked at me and asked , are you hungry? Tony , would you like me to fix you something to eat?. Something to eat? wait what? Something to eat? Tony thought , did she just ask if I wanted something to eat. Then she repeated it again.Tony rubbed his ears. I just stood there frozen. While Mama Lita was talking to Farmer Yarth, she kept cutting up vegetables and putting them in a big pot. And a few moments later all of these delicious smells kept coming into my nose. My head was spinning from the amazing smells. My mouth was watering. Oh no, I was drooling How embarrassing Tony thought.

I had never smelt anything like that before. When she was done, she put it in a big, huge shiny silver bowl. Farmer Yarth went to the other room to watch TV. Mama Lita brought me a silver bowl with the most delicious smell. She sat it right in front of me. She said here's your dinner. I'd never had my own bowl, and I certainly never got to have my own dinner. Tears of joy started to stream down my face. It was so delicious. I ate every single bit and licked the bowl. My tummy was so full. I was so happy and then remembered how much I missed Kody. Then I was sad again.

Later that evening, mama Lita and Farmer Yarth went into another room. Farmer Yarth was always playing games on his phone. He did not spend a lot of time with us. There was a bed for me. I'd never slept in a bed before. I had always slept outside in the tall grass with Kody. I lay in the warm, cozy bed as a smile came across my face. Then I wondered where my brother Kody was as I drifted off to sleep. When I woke up I thought I was dreaming. My bed was so comfy I didn't want to get up. In the morning farmer Yarth said to Mama Lita I'm going to pick up Kody and take him to Grandmother Joe. I closed my eyes and hoped that Grandmother Joe was as nice to Kody as Mama Lita was to me.

Mama Lita Said it was time to go for a walk. I had never seen anything so beautiful. The trees were very tall and the grass was very low and green. The smell was amazing. There were rows and rows of trees. We walked for a very long time, and Mama Lita kept saying , I hope you like it here Tony. I'm so happy you're here. We will keep each other company and go on lots of adventures. I didn't know what an adventure was , but if it was as good as the food , I was going to love it. In meanwhile Farmer Yarth had taken Kody to Grandma Joes. When Kody got to Grandma Joes. He jumped out of the truck and jumped up to say hello to Grandma Joe. Grandma Joe fell to the ground and Started screaming "TAKE HIM AWAY!"

I don't want him here! TAKE HIM AWAY NOW! Poor Kody was just trying to say hello. He didn't think Grandma Joe would fall. He would never hurt anyone. Farmer Yarth was so mad he put Kody in his truck. He drove so fast Kody was scared. He was silently crying. He didn't let farmer Yarth see him cry.

As Mama Lita and I were walking back from the field, we could hear Farmer Yarth's truck pull up. Mama Lita looked over at me and said he's not supposed to be done with work this early. Let's go see what's going on. As Farmer Yarth came closer, we could see Kody was with him. I was so happy to see my brother. Tears came down one eye. I tried to cover it with my paw. Farmer Yarth explained everything that had happened at Grandma Joe's. And he looked right at Mama Lita and said can Kody stay here until I find him a home? Mama Lita said he could stay here as long as he needed to. Or as long as Farmer Yarth wanted him to. I couldn't believe my ears. I was so excited. Then it was time to eat, and Mama Lita started to cook the yummy smelling food again. My stomach started to growl. I was hoping the food would be good again. It was even better , it was so delicious. Kody gobbled his food down. I had never seen my brother eat so fast. He finished his bowl in four huge bites.

Kody and I had our own beautiful silver dishes and our own water bowl. We each had our own beds. We were warm and safe and felt loved.

I couldn't believe how lucky Kody and I were. Every day was a new place to walk , play and sniff. Weekends were our favorite. We'd go in the car. To different places. Sniff new spots. Mama Lita would call this adventures. I learned that I loved adventures. Some days we got to see rivers. Other times it was lakes or canyons redwoods, mountains, beaches, and or snow. Kody and I loved every day with Mama Lita. Everwhere moma Lita went we would follow. We knew Mama Lita would protect and take care of us. We loved her and the almond orchards. Moma Lita would bring snacks and take us on hikes and picnics. We would play catch and run. As soon as it was morning we were ready to go. Moma Lita would say we were her pride and joy. She made us feel importan. Like we really mattered.

One day we drove for a long time, it felt like days. Moma Lita said we were going to meet family. I never had a family before. Unless you call living on the farm with Farmer Kurt family. It was always Kody and Lucy and I.

We had lots of family and that was great. Now it was time to meet them. Even though they were far away. Farmer Yarth brought us to his sister Meryl's house. Meryl lived with Sissy, Mom, and Jess in a beautiful house, way up on a hill. It was very cold and windy by the time we got there.

That day we met our cousins Flash and Bailey and lots more. There were so many nice people and all the different types of dogs. Some were tall and dark and others were short and light. Some with long hair. Others with short hair.

Aunt Meryl was a very nice firefighter and she taught Flash and Bailey how to have manners. They were very smart dogs. They never pushed or jumped on anyone. Sheriff Sissy taught them manners as well. That was when we learned not to push people when we ran. They also explained that jumping on people was not nice. She let us know we should not walk up to people and lick them. That is when we found out we had to start school. Momma Lita told us school was going to teach us how to behave around other people. We hoped for a nice teacher like aunt Myrle and aunt Sissy.

Mama Lita would always be so happy when Farmer Yarth came home. I loved walking through the fields and taking pictures with Moma Lita. Moma Lita was my favorite person.

Farmer Yarth got a call he started laughed and said "oh noooo. I'll be right over." I thought , what now to myself. He said to Mama Lita that there was a beautiful Dutch Shepherd that needed a home. Mama Lita said " go get her, we have room". That was the day we met Roxy. She was smaller than us but very pretty. She had course hair and a loud bark. It sounded funny coming from her. She was smaller but definitely strong and very fast. She was never scared. And liked to chase everything. Mama Lita said she would be our new sister. Roxy wasn't like our other sister. She was very nice. She loved to run and play. She never took our food. She played catch with us and loved to chase us . We learned to love her so much.

Farmer Yarth said that Kody and I needed to go to school. We needed to learn manners. So what happened at Grandma Joes would never happen again. One day we all drove for a long time. Until we got to a dog training school. That's when we met Amy , our teacher. She had brown hair and a strong voice. We learned Amy was the boss. We definitely listened to her. She and the other teachers taught us manners. They were strict but we loved them. They gave us treats when we were good. We always tried to be good. We love snacks.

On the weekends, Mama Lita would take us to classes. That way we wouldn't forget our manners. We learned a lot in school . Now we understood more of what Mama Lita and Farmer Yarth wanted us to do. The school was hard at times. I would forget things. Sometimes I would not do things right . I tried my very best.

Kody and I were the only German Shepherds that didn't have ears that stood up. People would sometimes talk about us and say mean thing that hurt our feelings. IMama Lita would say it doesn't matter what other people think, it only matters what you think. She also said that when you are different people can be mean because , they are afraid of things they don't understand,. It can also be that we are different than what they are use too. Mamma Lita took off her bright red bandana and lots of hair fell. Her hair was huge. I had never seen so much hair. She said I'm different too. When I was little people would make fun of my hair. It was not straight hair like everyone else's hair and it was thicker than most hair. At first I would try and hide it. I thought being different made me weird. I also didnt want people to laugh at me. Then as I grew older , Mamma Lita said , I learned I loved being different. She called herself unique.

Mamma Lita always reassured us that we were beautiful inside and out and we were very handsome. We were different but that's what made us special. Kody, Tony and Roxy and I graduated from school. Momma Lita was so proud. She hung our certificates on the wall. Mama Lita made sure to remind us daily of what we had learned , we would never forget.

It was a beautiful sunny day. I got up and ran to see Kody. Something was really wrong with him. He was laying down and he couldn't get up and he couldn't bark. He just looked at me with tears in his eyes.

The next few minutes went really fast, Mama grabbed Kody and put us in the car. We all went with Mama to a place called the hospital. They quickly took Kody inside the big building. Mama Lita was so sad and crying. I had never seen her like that. The doctor came out after what seemed to be hours. The animal doctor who was called a veterinarian. He told us that Kody was eating things he shouldn't be eating. I had told Kody over and over again not to eat the beds and not to eat stuff that he found. He would do it while no one was looking. He would sneak things in his mouth and eat them. Kody would say, I can't help it. It's a bad habit. When Mama Lita would shower he would sneak into the closet and grab socks and different things and eat them. It was not because they tasted good. Kody would just get nervous and eat things. He ate his new bed slowly so nobody would notice. I couldn't understand why, Kody would eat his soft new bed. I loved my bed. The veterinarian finally came out said Kody would have to stay in the animal hospital for a couple of days. Mama Lita was so sad. She sat down and started to cry. She would pace back and forth in the house holding the phone and waiting for any news about Kody it was a a day and then a night and another day. Finally, the phone rang. Kody was ok they had removed the blockage. They had taken everything out. He was going to come home. Moma Lita smiled for the first time in days.

Roxy and I couldn't wait for him to come home. We were not very happy with Kody. He had scared us. He made us worry. We told Kody that Farmer Yarth and Mama Lita only want the best for us. They didn't want us eating things for a good reason, If he didn't want to go to the animal hospital again, he should stop eating things that were bad. We hoped he would listen. He said he would.

It was a cold, windy day. When all of a sudden the phone rang. The person on the phone said that there is a boy dog named Taco. Who needed a home .We all thought that was a funny name for a dog. We had only known Tacos as a food to eat. We went down to this place , it was called a shelter . It kind of looked like a hospital, but it was cold and all the dogs were barking. They all looked at us with sad eyes. Some of them looked scared. Mama Lita said it is a place to go when you don't have a family or a home. I hoped everyone of them would find homes soon. They were all in cages. The lady who worked at the front desk showed us down this long cold hallway. That is when we met Taco. She said here you go and handed Farmer Yarth a beautiful Belgian Malinois dog. He had dark coloring, brown and reddish. His face was different than ours. He had a dark face. Mama Lita called it a mask. It look like a mask. Mama Lita said we're gonna change your name to Fury. From that day forward Taco was named Fury. I said to everyone 3plusfury. And that is how we got our family name.

Fury was very wild. He loved to run around. He especially liked Roxy. He was always chasing Roxy. They were always playing together. Our family had gone from one dog to four. I loved having lots of family. We visited family and went on adventures, took hikes, and did different fun things. We got to met our cousin, Tank. They called him a French bulldog. He ran around all the time, he never sat down, loved to boss us around. We got to go walking with Mila, Niko, and Gage they were little but lots of fun. Mama Lita would tell us they are children so please be extra careful with them and protect them. German Shepherds, and Dutch Shepherds, and Belgian Malinois are great protectors. We love our family and we're happy to have a job to do.

Kody Roxy and I got to stay home with Mama Lita. Fury is very active and does not like to be alone. He would go with farmer Yarth to work early in the morning. He would play while Farmer Yarth worked. Fury never took breaks. He would run from one side to the other all the time. It seemed like time went fast from that point on.

Every month was better than the last, and every day was better than the day before. It didn't matter that our ears didn't stand up. Because we had a home and we were loved.

It was Fury's s turn to go to school. Teacher Amy said he was a fast learner. She had taught all of us manners. Fury was a jumper and had to be told a couple of times before he listened. We loved when we went to school. We liked staying home, but we did like school too. Especially when we got treats for being good.

Farmer Yarth was getting busier and busier at work. He was not coming home as much. When he was home he would go straight to bed. When we got up Fury and Farmer Yarth would be gone to work. We hardly got to see them. Then one day Farmer Yarth just stopped coming home. Momma Lita would call but Farmer Yarth did not answer. She would say he's too busy to answer. Mama Lita was so very sad. She cried for days. We didn't understand why he would not call back. She would make us food and walk us and go right back to bed and cry. We asked her what we had done wrong, Mama Lita explained that we had done nothing wrong and that nothing was our fault but that there would be certain changes.

We didn't understand. We knew Mama Lita would take care of us and that's all that mattered. I didn't think I would like changes.

Mama Lita told us that Farmer Yarth was going to be living in a different house and Farmer Yarth was taking Fury with Him. We all stood there howling. We didn't like that. We just listened. I was so mad at Farmer Yarth. I wondered how he could do this to our family; how could he just leave us. Mama Lita said sometimes people need different things. People don't always tell you why. They just have to leave. It's not anyone's fault. It's not your fault. It's not my fault. It's not Farmer Yarth's fault. People can love each other and go in different directions. She also said, I should never be mad at Farmer Yarth if it wasn't for him. I wouldn't have you or Kody. We must always be grateful to Farmer Yarth. He brought us together. She could never thank him enough for that. He also helped take us to school and meet all the great teachers.

After a long time, farmer Yarth finally called and said we could come visit Fury on the weekends. This was great news. We just won't all be living together. Tony thought about all the things that had happened. I know in life, things change, We have to make the best of every day. Mama Lita was not sad from that point on. She was back to normal and we were back to our regular routine. Adventurous days with lots of fun.

All the trees had white leaves with pink little flowers. Mama Lita called them almond blossoms, some of the petals were on the floor. They looked like snow. Kody, Roxy, Fury, and I, all ran through the fields laughing. Tony smiled and Kody smiled back. It was a beautiful day, full of love. Everything was going to be ok. I thought to myself. Different does not have to be bad, neither does change. That was a hard lesson. One I was glad to learn from.

Later that day we found out that Jerrica, Helena, and Remy, our family far away, were getting a new puppy. They named her Layla. They said she was an Australian Shepherd. I realized at that moment life changed all the time. That it was ok to be sad sometimes, but not to stay sad. To always look for the good things in life. That if your different that you should be proud. That good things are just around the corner. And that life is beautiful . And being loved is the greatest thing.

The End!

That is how we became 3plusfury. If you would like to see more of our adventures or the places we visit, please come see us on Instagram or TikTok.

Stayed tuned for Fury 2.

We love you.

www.ingramcontent.com/pod-product-compliance
Lightning Source LLC
LaVergne TN
LVHW072131070426

835513LV00002B/69